© BRITT ALLCROFT LIMITED 1983

Published by

 BUDGET BOOKS PTY. LTD.

PUBLISHERS & BOOK DISTRIBUTORS (INCORPORATED IN VICTORIA)

ISBN 0 86801 924 0.

Published by Budget Books Pty Ltd 1987.
Printed in Korea by Dong-A Printing
Re-printed 1988

© Kaye & Ward Ltd. 1984, 1986.
© Britt Allcroft Ltd. 1984, 1986.

Based on the Railway series by The Rev. W. Awdry
Photographic stills by David Mitton and Terry Permane from the TV series
Thomas the Tank Engine and Friends.
© Britt Allcroft Ltd. 1984, 1986.

Written by Christopher Awdry. Word Search and Word Place puzzle ideas
supplied by Jean Mintoft. Text stories and game illustrations
by David Palmer (Temple Art). Black and white illustrations by Owain Bell.
All illustrations © 1986 Kaye & Ward Ltd.
© 1986 Britt Allcroft Ltd. All photographs © 1986 Britt Allcroft Ltd.
Originally published by Grandreams Limited,
London.

MELBOURNE AUSTRALIA

To James, Happy Birthday, 1988
love from
Sue, Peter, Nicholas, Caitlyn
and Elizabeth.

Contents

Hello!

Hello Everybody,
I'm Boco, and there's a special reason why I'm introducing this new Thomas the Tank Engine & Friends Annual. I've discovered that there's another engine like me!

Well, perhaps 'discovered' is going a bit too far, but I thought all engines like me had been scrapped, and now Mr. Awdry tells me they haven't. It seems he (the engine, not Mr. Awdry) had been stored at a place called Swindon — you know, that place which Duck and Oliver are always going on about.

It was a splendid surprise for me, as you can imagine. When we both worked for British Railways, the engine's number was D5705; we used to work together on the Mainland, not far from here. Sometimes we used to pass a narrow-gauge line at Ravenglass, called the Ravenglass and Eskdale Railway. There's one like it on Sodor, but I don't have the chance to visit it I'm afraid — Duck and Oliver do all the work

in that direction.

But I was telling you about my engine friend; he's at Matlock in Derbyshire now, where enthusiasts are restoring him. The Fat Controller says that the people there want to re-open a railway. It sounds exciting doesn't it? But re-opening railways takes a lot of money and hard work, so I expect it will be a little while before D5705 is running again.

Anyway, for the time being, here are some more stories about engines who are running. I hope you will enjoy these stories — I certainly did.

BOCO

Donald and The Lost Tarpaulin

Donald and Douglas help with the goods traffic on Duck's branch line. In the summer, when the weather is fine, they enjoy it, but they don't like it so much when it is wet. No engine likes being rained on (Henry had even stayed in a tunnel once, to avoid it), but there is no turntable at the end of Duck's branch, so that tender engines always have to travel backwards in one direction.

"It's no' guid enough," grumbled Donald to Duck one wet day. "Why canna' the Fat Controller put a turntable up here, eh?"

"He probably doesn't think it's worth it, just for Oliver and me," replied Duck.

"Humph!" snorted Donald. "He ought to try riding in a cab on a day like this. It's a' richt for you — you've a proper back to your cab that keeps the rain awa' when it's coming doon in torrents. Dougie an' me hae naethin'."

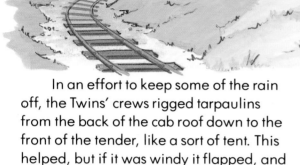

In an effort to keep some of the rain off, the Twins' crews rigged tarpaulins from the back of the cab roof down to the front of the tender, like a sort of tent. This helped, but if it was windy it flapped, and made itself a nuisance.

But, at last, the weather improved. It did so suddenly, at a time when Donald's driver and fireman had to make a quick turnround at the Big Station. The fireman only had time to bundle the tarpaulin roughly into a roll and put it out of the way on the back of the tender. Then, they hurried to the Yard to take water for the next journey.

Just before they set out with their goods train, the fireman, who was shovelling coal forward from the back of the tender, noticed that the tarpaulin had disappeared.

"Did you move it?" he asked the driver.

The driver shook his head.

"Haven't seen it since you took it down," he said.

"Bother!" said the fireman. "It must have fallen off in the Yard. Let's hope it doesn't rain again before we find it."

They reached Arlesburgh safely, but on the way back had to wait outside the middle station.

"I'm thirsty," Donald complained, after a while.

His driver opened his injector, but no water came from the tender into the boiler.

"Try yours," the driver told the fireman. He did, but it made no difference.

"Ooooooh!" groaned Donald. "I've got such a pain!"

"Your injectors have failed," said his driver. "There's nothing for it but to drop your fire and then try and repair it."

Meanwhile, Donald's fireman had climbed to the back of the tender to check the level of the water in the tank. He lifted the filler-cap and peered in.

"Well I'll be..!" he exclaimed. "So that's where our tarpaulin went!"

Seizing a long steel pole he plunged it into the water and managed to pull the sodden tarpaulin away from the feedpipe which it was blocking. Water was soon flowing merrily into Donald's boiler once more, but when they reached the Yard the

driver and fireman had a hard job getting
the tarpaulin out of the tank. When they
finished they were very wet, very hot and
very cross. The fireman vowed never to
store the tarpaulin near the water filler
again. The driver intends to make sure he
doesn't!

A Picture to Colour

12

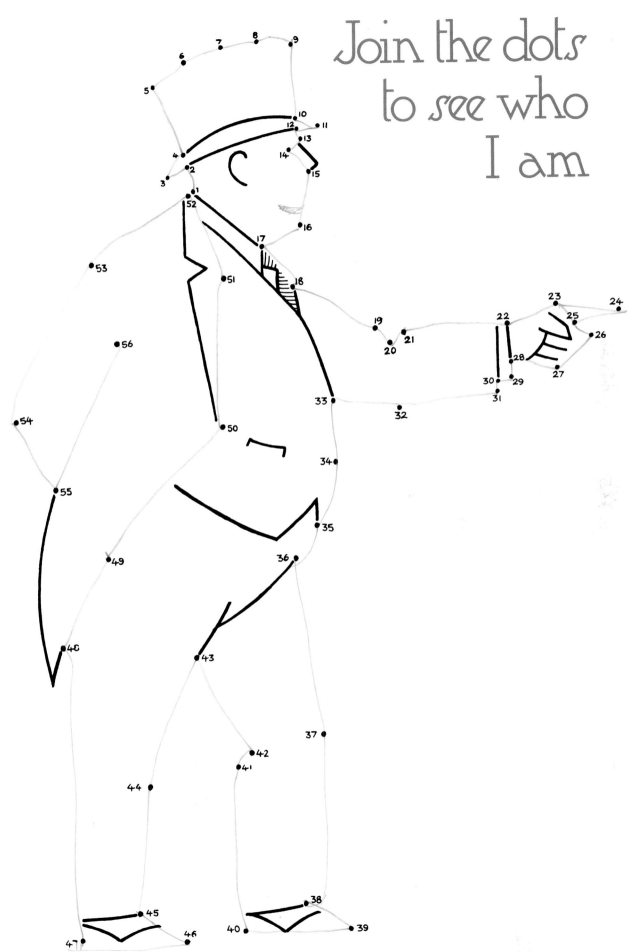

Join the dots to see who I am

13

Daisy

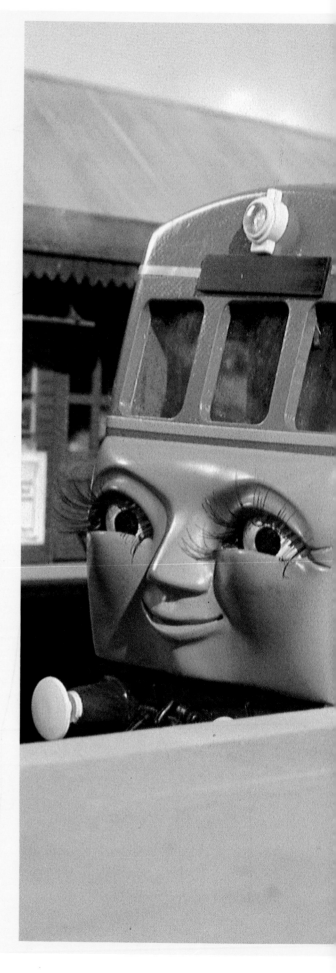

Daisy was built specially for service on Thomas's branch line. Thomas, you may remember, thought he could manage without his driver and one morning he wanted to frighten Percy and Toby as they dozed in the Shed. "I'll just go out and then I'll stop and 'wheesh', that'll make them jump," he said. But what Thomas didn't know was that a careless cleaner had meddled with his controls and when he tried to 'wheesh', he couldn't and when he tried to stop, he couldn't. Poor Thomas kept on going and then he crashed into the stationmaster's house just when the Fat Controller was having breakfast. It was while Thomas was having the damage caused by the accident repaired that Daisy was brought in to do his work.

Daisy was rather conceited at first and although she became a reformed character, she still has her fads. She has a very strong objection to pulling anything, and though she will, in an emergency, do her bit, she is still rather inclined to leave the milk van for someone else to clear up. The someone else usually turns out to be Percy, which doesn't improve his temper! But Daisy's heart is in the right place, and though she is frequently teased about bulls, she now takes it all in good part. She knows that the only efficient way to run a railway is the Fat Controller's way, and she does her best to keep things as he would wish.

Railway

1. How many wheels has Gordon got ?
2. Gordon once had a very special visitor. Who was he ?

3. Who banged his coaches so hard that they had to be mended with newspaper and a leather bootlace ?

4. Where do Bill and Ben work ?

5. Which engine is Number 3 ?

Quiz

6. Who once fell down a mine . . .

7. and who pulled him out of it?

him

8. Who rescued Thomas
and the Christmas Tree
from a snowdrift?

him

9. What number is Percy?

perry

10. Who once had a race with
Thomas?

Answers on pages 60-61.

Draw a picture of Diesel in the space below, using the squares as a guide. Then colour both pictures in.

18

There are 10 differences between these two pictures. Can you spot them? Answers on pages 60-61.

19

Bill and Ben

Bill and Ben are identical twins, which can sometimes be very confusing for their owner.

But did you know that once there were two engines very much like Bill and Ben? They used to work on China Clay trains at Par, in Cornwall. They were called Alfred and Judy, and, like them, Bill and Ben are low-slung 0-4-0 saddle-tank engines, built by W. F. Bagnall's, of Stafford, in 1948. Bill and Ben belong to the Sodor China Clay Company, and work on the Company's private railway between the clay pits and the harbour at Brendam, which is also the end of Edward's branch line.

Edward and Boco are the engines on the Fat Controller's Railway who have the most to do with the Twins. Edward has no trouble keeping them in order, but to begin with, Boco didn't know their ways. He soon learned, however, and was able to save Gordon from an unpleasant experience once, when Gordon was sent along the wrong line by mistake. Gordon still believes that Boco saved his life...who knows? Maybe he did! Down at Par, Alfred and Judy are retired now and one of them lives in a museum, but Bill and Ben still have plenty to do, and seem likely to go on working for many more years yet.

James was hurrying to get home. A late connection on the Other Railway had made him miss his path, and this had led to more hold-ups all the way along the line. Now, at last, the track in front of him seemed to be free from obstructions, and as he came fast down Gordon's Hill the signals at Edward's station were all showing clear.

He raced along the platform and was about half way along when a signal a few yards in front of him suddenly moved back to danger.

"Whoa, James," said the driver, and put the brakes hard on.

"Botheration!" said James. "Just when we'd got moving nicely, too."

James, of course, was going much too fast to stop before the signal and was some way past when he finally came to a halt.

The fireman got down and walked back to the signalbox while James stood simmering crossly.

"Stupid signal!" he muttered. "Might have caused an accident, making us stop quickly like that."

"Now, James," said his driver soothingly. "There might have been an even worse accident if we hadn't stopped."

After a while the fireman came back.

"Runaway truck at the next station," he reported. "They've cleared it now — look, the signal's down."

James set off again, but was, of course, very late at the Big Station.

The signalman reported, as he had to, that James had passed a signal at danger.

"You must be more careful, James," the Fat Controller told him.

"But Sir..." protested James.

"That's enough, James," said the Fat

Controller. "Just remember what I've said. It is a very serious matter, whatever the reason." He walked sternly away.

"It's not fair," grumbled James in the Shed that night. "Signals are stupid things anyway. Get on a whole lot better without them, if you ask me."

Percy was puzzled.

"But surely they're there to make things safer, aren't they?" he asked.

"Pooh!" scoffed James. "Just a nuisance, that's all."

"All the same, I'd like to see how you'd manage without them," put in Edward with a smile.

"Probably a good deal faster," boasted James loftily.

But he spoke too soon.

That night the wind increased, and by morning a full force gale was screaming across the Island. At the Junction the gusts became fiercer, until

24

Thomas, waiting with Annie and Clarabel, grew alarmed. The wind swept under the station canopy, and the building rocked. Leaves and small branches, driven by the wind, hit Thomas's front.

"Ouch!" he exclaimed. "That hurt."

"Come on, Thomas," said the driver. "I don't like the look of that canopy. Let's draw forward to the signal, so that if it does fall it won't land on us or our passengers."

He warned the Guard what he was going to do, and eased open Thomas's regulator. Thomas moved slowly forward: he was just about to stop at the signal when, with a whistling and a swoosh, a fierce gust ripped along the platform. There was a sharp crack and the signal disappeared.

One moment it was standing upright, its arm at danger, the next it was lying beside the line, its lamp shattered and its

wires flying out like streamers.

"That's torn it," said Thomas's
fireman. He looked back towards the
platform. As he watched, three more
signals rocked and fell, and part of the
station canopy lifted clean off its
framework, to shatter, with a crash, on the
platform below.

"Wow!" he exclaimed. "Let's get out
of here!"

"We daren't," said the driver. "Not

with our signal gone. Nip back to the
signalbox and find out what's to do."

The fireman was gone for some time.
He came back looking glum.

"Signalman's got power," he said,
"but he's lost all his signals. Control has
cancelled everything until flagmen can
get out, but I got permission for us to go
since our road's set. We'll be the last for a
while, I reckon."

He was right. Things were at a

standstill for some time, but at last, men with red and green flags were posted wherever signals guarded crossings or points. Drivers were all instructed to proceed at caution, until they were shown a green flag at each place. It meant slow going, but at least the trains were moving again.

James was first through. He had to stop twice before he reached the platform and he grumbled like anything. As he stopped, Edward arrived from the other direction.

"Won't it be nice when we get our signals back," he remarked brightly. "You're late today, James — I thought you got on faster without signals to hold you up. Feeling all right, are you?"

James snorted, and at that moment the flagman in front of him showed a green flag. James went, as quickly as he dared.

Join the dots to see who I am

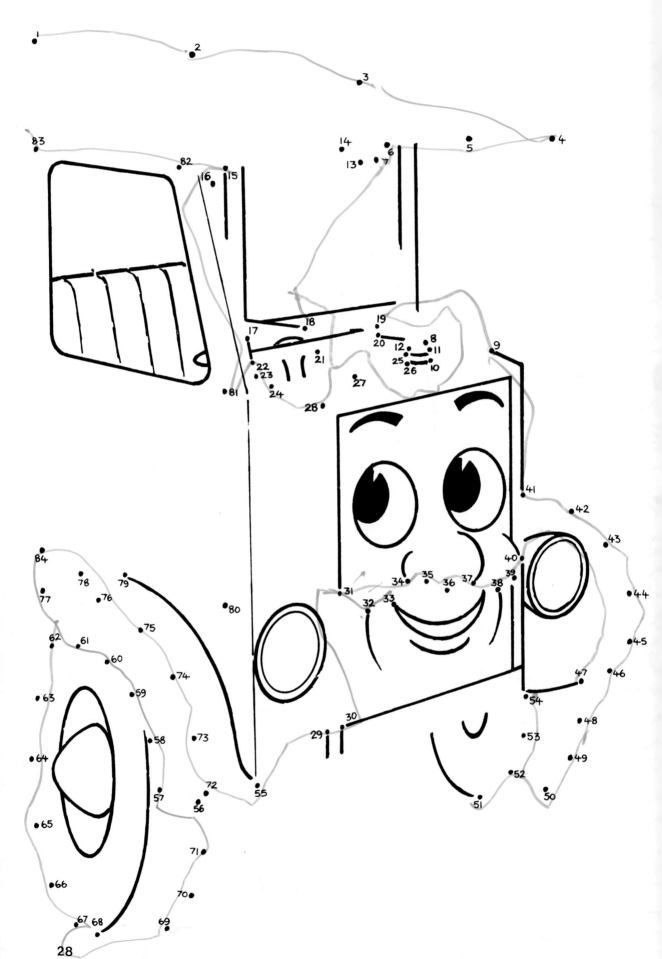

A Picture to Colour

Diesel

Some years ago, when the Fat Controller had a problem with shunting in the Yard at Tidmouth, he asked the Other Railway if they could help. They sent a black 0-6-0 diesel-shunter which the Fat Controller agreed to take on trial. 'Trial', he admitted afterwards, described the experience exactly! When Diesel arrived he was oily but polite. The Fat Controller gave Duck the job of showing Diesel around, but Diesel didn''t want to be shown around. He was so conceited about how revolutionary he was, that all he really wanted to do was show off. Duck decided to take him down a peg or two, and in return Diesel spread untrue stories about the other engines, pretending that the stories came from Duck.

But the Fat Controller wasn't fooled. He sent Duck away, and in doing so allowed Diesel enough fuel in which to drown himself. Even after Duck's departure the stories went on, because Diesel was too conceited to stop, proving that it had not been Duck who started them in the first place. As soon as Diesel was sent packing, the stories finished. Duck came back to the Yard again, and I'm pleased to say that there has been no similar trouble since.

Railway Ups and Downs

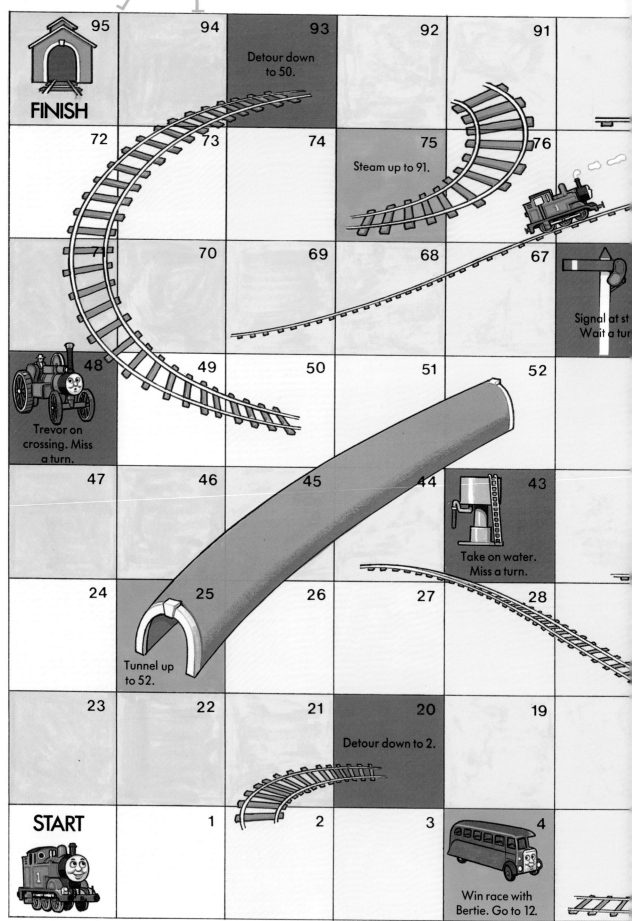

95 FINISH	94	93 Detour down to 50.	92	91
72	73	74	75 Steam up to 91.	76
71	70	69	68	67
48 Trevor on crossing. Miss a turn.	49	50	51	52
47	46	45	44	43 Take on water. Miss a turn.
24	25 Tunnel up to 52.	26	27	28
23	22	21	20 Detour down to 2.	19
START	1	2	3	4 Win race with Bertie. Go to 12.

Signal at st
Wait a tur

You need a counter for each player, a dice and a shaker. Roll the dice and move your counter the number shown. If you land on a square with instructions, do what they say. Throw an exact number to finish. The first to square 95 is the winner.

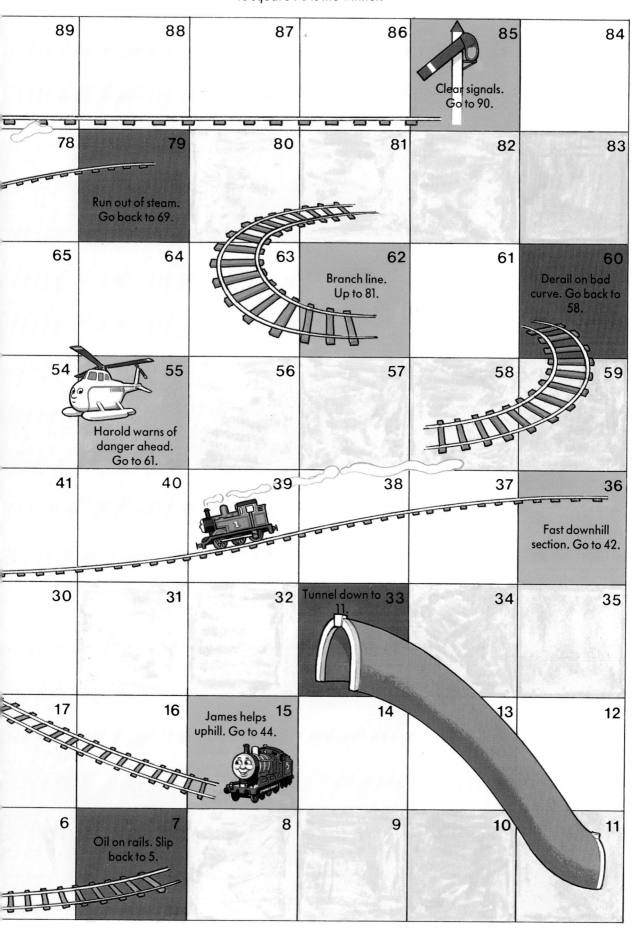

89	88	87	86	85 Clear signals. Go to 90.	84
78	79 Run out of steam. Go back to 69.	80	81	82	83
65	64	63	62 Branch line. Up to 81.	61	60 Derail on bad curve. Go back to 58.
54	55 Harold warns of danger ahead. Go to 61.	56	57	58	59
41	40	39	38	37	36 Fast downhill section. Go to 42.
30	31	32	33 Tunnel down to 11.	34	35
17	16	15 James helps uphill. Go to 44.	14	13	12
6	7 Oil on rails. Slip back to 5.	8	9	10	11

33

Timber!

On the village green at Wellsworth there stood an enormous old elm tree. One autumn night a great gale blew and broke off one of the branches, which crashed heavily to the ground. No-one was hurt, but there was an awful mess.

Next day, men came and inspected the tree. They measured this and that and made important-looking notes on their pads, nodding and looking serious.

"It's not safe," they said to each other. "It'll have to come down."

A day was fixed, and it happened that on the same day, Jem Cole and Trevor were working in the Vicarage garden, cutting a supply of logs to last the Vicar through the winter.

Trevor is an old green traction engine. Some years ago, Edward helped to save him from the scrapyard; he persuaded the Vicar to buy him, and now Trevor lives in the Vicar's orchard. In winter he saws logs for the Vicarage fires, and in summer he gives children rides whenever he is asked to do so. Jem Cole, his driver, is always glad when the Vicar says there is work for Trevor.

"Trevor and me make a good partnership," he says.

Trevor and Jem had been busy all morning, and a great pile of cut logs showed that they had almost finished. Suddenly, they heard a shout from the gate. Jem carefully stopped the saw and went to find out what was the matter. He came back with a great grin right across his face.

"The tree cutter on the Green has broken down," he said, "and they want to borrow you, Trevor, my lad. I'd better go and find the Reverence." He hurried away.

The Vicar was delighted to let Trevor help.

"I wish I could come too, but my sermon will never get finished if I do," he said.

The Green wasn't far away, and soon Trevor and Jem had reached the crowd waiting for them. Jem drove Trevor into position and made his saw ready, a bigger one this time. Then he pulled the lever and Trevor chuffed happily.

The old tree trunk was thick, and it took some while to cut through it. But at last the tree creaked, leaned a little way and stopped. Jem stretched out a brawny arm and pushed it, very gently.

"Timber!" shouted someone.

The great elm tree leaned further and further, until, with a crack and a roar, it toppled to the ground. Debris flew in all directions, and a great cloud of rooks, cawing crossly at being disturbed, rose from the trees nearby and drifted about in the air like pieces of burnt paper.

Trevor and Jem spent all next day cutting the fallen giant into smaller lengths and dragging them close to the road where a lorry could collect them. Then at last, the job well done, Trevor chuffered happily back to his place in the Vicarage orchard.

"I enjoyed that," he said to himself. "Just like the old days."

And with a happy smile on his face he fell asleep.

A Picture to Colour

There are 10 differences between these two pictures. Can you spot them? Answers on pages 60-61.

Thomas's Word Search

On the page opposite are **9** characters associated with Thomas The Tank Engine, whose names are hidden in the grid below. All the words can be found in straight lines — but they can be found in any direction. Answers on pages 60-61.

D	A	C	K	R	L	E	D	W	A	R	D	T	X	H
A	S	Y	P	N	J	N	B	E	I	O	J	F	T	E
C	F	M	O	Y	A	X	E	T	O	B	Y	H	U	N
P	G	T	H	O	M	A	S	K	L	S	G	P	O	R
S	D	R	K	T	E	T	C	W	B	E	N	G	F	I
B	I	L	L	Z	S	J	A	Y	L	M	N	T	O	E
K	A	T	M	B	H	P	E	R	C	Y	Q	B	L	T
F	A	T	C	O	N	T	R	O	L	L	E	R	S	T
N	A	C	O	R	A	V	D	Z	B	F	C	G	L	A

James

Bill

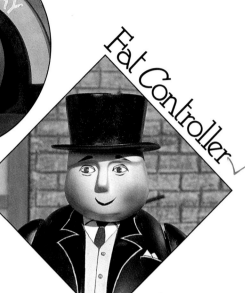

Fat Controller ✓

Toby and Henrietta ✓

Ben

Thomas

Edward ✓

Percy ✓

Lost In The Snow

Thomas's driver and fireman watched the sky anxiously. Heavy clouds loomed and lowered, and it became dusk in the middle of the day.

"We're in for it," said the driver. "We'll be needing the snowplough before long."

Thomas was cross. He didn't like the snowplough. It was heavy and cumbersome, but he remembered that Terence had had to come and pull him out of a snowdrift when he'd been silly about it before.

"I shall just have to put up with it, I suppose," he said to himself.

His driver was right. Before long it was snowing, and by next morning the countryside was thickly covered. Thomas could not go as fast as usual, and his fireman wanted to top up his watertanks at the Junction. But they found that the water column was out of order.

"Never mind, Thomas," he said. "We can last until the station by the airfield — we'll get some water there."

Among the passengers who got into Annie at the Junction was a lady carrying a large basket. Inside the basket was something which moved about, and now and then mewed faintly.

"I'm taking my cat to my daughter's," explained the woman. "She's going to look after him for me when I go away at Christmas."

Once the train was safely on the move the lady opened the basket, and everyone made a great fuss of the cat as he sat on his owner's lap.

Thomas stopped at the station by the airfield, and several passengers got out. A door slammed. The cat was startled. With a swift look round, he jumped off the lady's lap, through an open window and disappeared into the snow outside.

"Oh no!" wailed the woman, and

getting out of Annie herself, ran to find the Guard.

"Not to worry," he said encouragingly. "Thomas needs water, so we shall have to spend a few minutes here in any case. You've time to look for your cat — he can't have gone far in this snow."

Some of the other passengers got out to help with the search. Thomas's driver and fireman got out too, but they didn't help. They had troubles of their own: the water column here was frozen too like the one at the Junction, and by now the water level in Thomas's tanks was getting dangerously low.

"Where's your shovel?" the driver asked the fireman. "We'll have to fill the tank with snow."

Thomas shivered, but said nothing.

He knew that the alternative was even worse.

The fireman clambered on to the top of Thomas's tank, and the driver passed a shovel up to him. Then he took his place on the ground, and began throwing shovelfulls of snow up, aiming to land them on the tank beside the fireman. Not all the snow reached its target, and each time some hit his boiler, Thomas shuddered.

"Sorry, Thomas," said his driver cheerfully. "Some children go snow-balling for fun, you know."

"Brrrrrrrr," muttered Thomas to himself. "Not my idea of fun."

Meanwhile, down on the ground, the searchers for the cat were growing desperate. They seemed to have looked everywhere, but the animal couldn't be

found. He was not on the station, in the train, under the train or anywhere near it. They even looked in Thomas's cab, but he wasn't there either.

Just then there was a shout from outside.

"Nearly full," called the fireman.

The driver mopped his brow.

"Thank goodness for that!" he remarked. "This is warm work."

He slid the shovel once more under a heap of snow, and lifted. The snow on the shovel moved: the driver almost dropped it in surprise. Then the heap of snow mewed.

"Well I'm blessed!" exclaimed the driver. "What a good job we didn't put that into Thomas's tank!"

They went to find the stationmaster, who gave them an old towel. Then, when the cat had been thoroughly dried, a porter gave her some warmed milk, and the cat's owner thankfully put her animal back in his basket.

Later, in the Shed, Thomas told Percy and Toby about the adventure.

"I'm glad the lady got her cat back," he said. "Now she can go away and have a happy Christmas after all. But I'll tell you something else," he added, "take my advice and never go snowballing. It's no fun at all — I've tried it, so I know."

46

Draw a picture of Thomas in the space below, using the squares as a guide. Then colour both pictures in.

1	2	3	4	5	6	7	8	P
18	11	18	B	D	1	/	/	
10	D1	12	21	23	21	12	12	12
31	34	43	58	78	7P	78	rc	8P
B	P	o	+	T	l	i	e	S
h	D	W	R	S	T	i	e	S

Annie and Clarabel

Annie and Clarabel have probably been on the Island of Sodor as long as Thomas has, but Thomas didn't meet them until, as a reward for proving himself a Really Useful Engine, the Fat Controller gave him his branch line. Annie only carries passengers, but Clarabel is a 'composite' coach, and has two sections, one for passengers, and the other for luggage and the Guard.

It is most likely that Annie and Clarabel were bought second-hand from one of the railways on the Mainland many years ago when the railways on Sodor were being built. They are wooden-bodied coaches, similar in construction to many six-wheelers built early this century. Possibly they were lengthened and converted from six-wheelers to bogie coaches after they came to the Island, and if this is so it is likely that they began life with oil-lamps to light their compartments. The Fat Controller saw to it that this old-fashioned system was properly changed to electricity, but although they are old, Annie and Clarabel are still more than capable of a good day's work. No matter how tired they feel, their motto has always been: 'We mustn't let Thomas down'.

Join the dots to see who I am

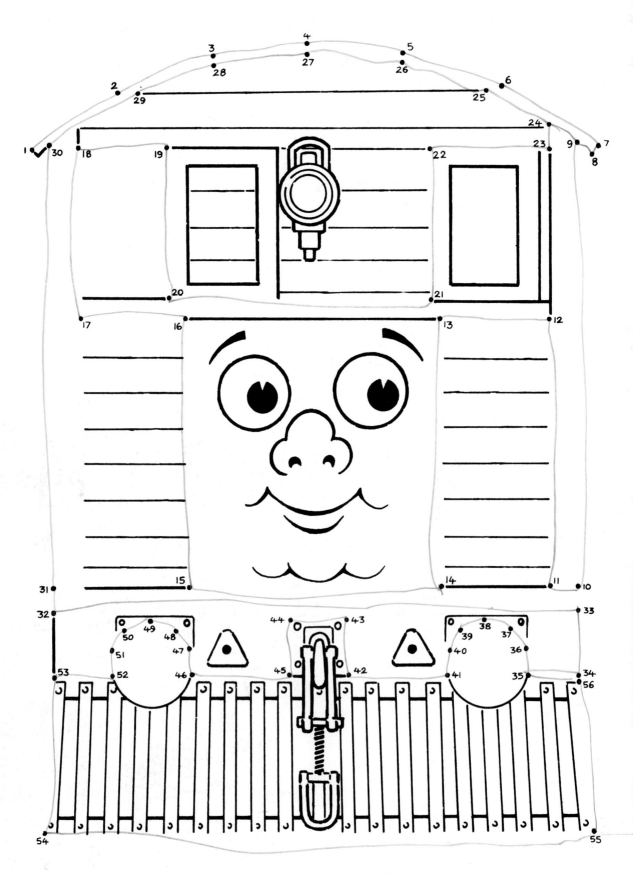

A Picture to Colour

Percy's Passengers

Percy was talking to James in the Shed at the Big Station. "My Guard was telling me how lonely he is in his van," he was saying. "I think he ought to take passengers sometimes, to cheer him up."

"He's not allowed to," said James virtuously. "It's against regulations. Guards are important, and passengers might distract them so that they couldn't look after the train properly."

"Oh dear!" said Percy. "Yes, I suppose they might."

"They do it on the Midland," put in Gordon. "Someone told me about it when I went to Carlisle with that Special. But they don't do it on the Other Railway — it's on some preserved lines where they haven't got any coaches."

"You see, James," said Percy triumphantly.

"Oh well, if they haven't got any coaches, that's different," said James huffily. "I'm sure the Fat Controller wouldn't approve."

"Pooh!" replied Percy cheekily. "Little you know."

He puffed away to collect some trucks from the Harbour.

Meanwhile, on the branch line, some passengers got out of Henrietta at the station by the airfield. They all went through the ticket barrier except for two, a man and a woman.

"Ah!" said the ticket inspector when he looked at their tickets. "You've come too far, I'm afraid, Sir. You should have got out at the last station."

The two people looked at him. Then they looked at each other and shook their heads.

"The last station," repeated the ticket inspector, slowly. "You must go back."

There was a pause. Then the man said something to his wife in a language that the ticket inspector didn't understand a word of. He asked a porter to bring the stationmaster.

A short time later, Percy came

chuntering happily along the branch line with his trucks from the Harbour. He saw the signal at the station by the airfield at danger, and the stationmaster waiting on the platform.

"There must have been an accident," he thought as he stopped. "I hope nobody's hurt."

The stationmaster came over, with two other people.

"I'm giving the Guard these two passengers to travel in his van," he told Percy. "They're foreigners who came too far on Toby's train by mistake. Will you stop at the station by the river to let them off please?"

Percy was puzzled.

"Passengers?" he asked, when the Guard had taken them away. "But this is a goods train."

"That's right, Percy," said the stationmaster. "They're going to travel with the Guard in his van."

"But... James says it's against reg...er...it's not allowed, Sir."

The stationmaster laughed.

"Quite right, Percy," he said. "So it is, but I don't think James or the Fat Controller would mind us helping two foreign visitors on our Island, who can't understand our language, do you?"

That made it all right, of course. The Guard saw that his visitors were as comfortable as he could make them in his van, and when, a few minutes later, they reached the station they wanted, they came to the front of the train to see Percy. They nodded and smiled and shook hands with the driver and fireman. Then the Guard showed them to a taxi that was waiting to take them on the rest of their journey.

A few weeks later, a parcel arrived with brightly coloured foreign stamps on the wrapping. Inside were warm new scarves and gloves for Percy's driver, fireman and Guard, and a letter addressed to the Fat Controller, saying how splendid his Railway was.

Percy didn't tell James.

"It might make him jealous," Percy said to himself. "That would never do."

Harold
the Helicopter

It seems a very strange thing, but the idea for a machine like the helicopter is very old, older than the steam engine. It was 'invented' 500 years ago by an Italian artist called Leonardo da Vinci: modern experts believe that his design, though sound, would not have had enough power to lift its weight. But in more recent times, a Russian named Igor Sikorsky was experimenting with a helicopter in 1911: the idea, though, was not fully developed until 1939, by which time Sikorsky was living in America.

Harold the Helicopter came to live at an airfield near Thomas's branch line in 1956, and Percy was the first of the Fat Controller's engines to meet him. He thought Harold was noisy, describing him to Thomas as a sort of 'whirlybird' thing: Harold, for his part, boasted about how up-to-date he was — until Percy challenged him to a race, and won! But Harold proved how useful he could be a little later, when Percy became stranded in a flood, and Harold was able to help by parachuting hot drinks to Percy's passengers. Engine and helicopter have been firm friends since.

Thomas's Word Place

Can you fit the words listed below the silhouette of Thomas in the correct places in the engine? Answers on pages 60-61.

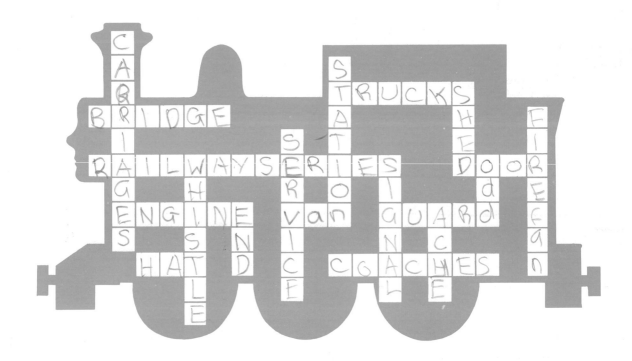

3 letters	4 letters	5 letters	6 letters
HAT	ACHE	GUARD	ENGINE
VAN	DOOR		BRIDGE
ODD	SHED		TRUCKS
END			SIGNAL

7 letters	9 letters	13 letters
STATION	CARRIAGES	RAILWAY SERIES
COACHES		
FIREMAN		
SERVICE		
WHISTLE		

Draw the picture in the space below, using the squares as a guide. Then colour both pictures in.

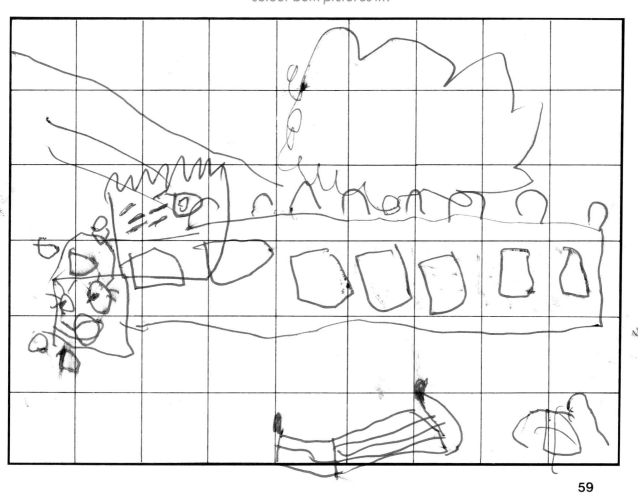

Answers

SPOT THE DIFFERENCE

Word Search

D	A	C	K	R	L	E	D	W	A	R	D	T	X	H
A	S	Y	P	N	J	N	B	E	I	O	J	F	T	E
C	F	M	O	Y	A	X	E	T	O	B	Y	H	U	N
P	G	T	H	O	M	A	S	K	L	S	G	P	O	R
S	D	R	K	T	E	T	C	W	B	E	N	G	F	I
B	I	L	L	Z	S	J	A	Y	L	M	N	T	O	E
K	A	T	M	B	H	P	E	R	C	Y	Q	B	L	T
F	A	T	C	O	N	T	R	O	L	L	E	R	S	T
N	A	C	O	R	A	V	D	Z	B	F	C	G	L	A

Railway Quiz

1. 12 (18 with tender), 2. Flying Scotsman,
3. James, 4. Brendam China Clay Works,
5. Henry, 6. Thomas, 7. Gordon, 8. Donald
and Douglas, 9. 6, 10. Bertie.

Word Place

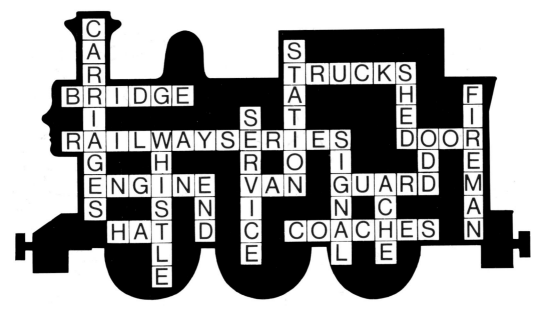